This book
belongs to

....

Other books by Mick Inkpen

KIPPER

KIPPER'S TOYBOX

KIPPER'S BIRTHDAY

KIPPER'S BOOK OF COLOURS

KIPPER'S BOOK OF COUNTING

KIPPER'S BOOK OF OPPOSITES

KIPPER'S BOOK OF WEATHER

ONE BEAR AT BEDTIME

THE BLUE BALLOON

THREADBEAR

BILLY'S BEETLE

LULLABYHULLABALLOO!

WHERE, OH WHERE, IS KIPPER'S BEAR?

British Library Cataloguing in Publication data

A catalogue record for this book
is available from the British Library.

ISBN 0 340 61935 X

Text and illustrations copyright © Mick Inkpen 1992

The right of Mick Inkpen to be identified as the author
of this work has been asserted by him in accordance with
the Copyright, Designs and Patents Act 1988.

First published 1992
Paperback edition first published 1994
20 19 18 17 16 15 14 13

Published by Hodder Children's Books,
a division of Hodder Headline plc,
338 Euston Road, London   NW1 3BH

Printed in Hong Kong

Penguin Small

Mick Inkpen

Hodder
Children's
Books

A division of Hodder Headline plc

The polar bears had been up to their nasty tricks again, and the North Pole penguins had had enough. They were off to the South Pole, to make their home where no polar bears could bully them.

Penguin Small watched his friends plop into the ocean and swim away.

'Come on!' they shouted. 'You can do it!' But Penguin Small wouldn't. He couldn't. He was terrified of water.

He always had been.

Penguin Small watched until his friends
disappeared among the bobbing waves.
Then he put his head under his wing and
cried until the tears made a long icicle on
the end of his beak.

   After a while he wandered off along the
water's edge, staring down at his feet and
sniffing loudly.

   He did not see the Snowman, which
is why he bumped into him.

'You weren't there yesterday,' said Penguin Small. 'Did the Eskimos make you?'

'What are Eskimos?' said the Snowman, who had been made only that morning, and had not yet learned many words.

'And what is yesterday?' he said. 'And what are those?'

Penguin Small turned and gave a frightened squeak. The polar bears were coming!

'Let me hide under your hat,' squeaked Penguin Small.

'What's a hat?' said the Snowman. Without answering Penguin Small hopped on to the Snowman's arm, then on to his shoulder, and up on to his head. He lifted the hat and crawled underneath.

'Sssh!' he whispered.

'Sssshhh?' repeated the Snowman loudly. Penguin Small reached down and rubbed out the Snowman's mouth with his flipper.

The polar bears were in a terrible mood.

'Where are the penguins?' said the first.
The Snowman said nothing.

'Where are the penguins?' growled the second.
The Snowman said nothing.

'TELL US WHERE THEY ARE!' roared the third.
And he began to thump the snow with his great
paws. Still the Snowman said nothing.

Soon all three bears were jumping up and down
in a rage. The ice groaned and creaked under them.

With a loud crack, the Snowman broke away
from the shore and floated away
on his own little iceberg.

'Serves you right!'
roared the bears.

They floated out to sea until the North Pole was left far behind. For days the little iceberg drifted south.

Penguin Small drew a new mouth for the Snowman and, to pass the time, he taught him all the words he knew.

Each day the sky grew brighter and the air warmer. But the Snowman did not melt. He was made of North Pole snow and, as anyone will tell you, the snow that falls at the North Pole never melts.

At last an island appeared on the horizon.

The island was a wonderful place.
    'It's full of junglybirds!' said the
Snowman, who had begun to make up words
of his own. They had never seen Threecans
before. Nor heard Hootercrabs. Nor made
friends with a Neverwozanoceros.

The Neverwozanoceros spent his time drawing. For each animal that appeared in the forest there was a picture on the rocks. There were hundreds of them.

'This jungland is a wonderful place!' said the Snowman. 'I want to stay here for ever.'

But Penguin Small began to miss his friends.

The Snowman did not want
Penguin Small to go. But he gave
him his hat for a boat when the time
came to say goodbye.

A teardrop trickled from his eye
and froze on his cheek as he pushed
Penguin Small out to sea.

'If only I could swim,' he said to the Neverwozanoceros one day.

'Perhaps you should fly,' said the Neverwozanoceros.

'Penguins can't fly!' said Penguin Small.

The Neverwozanoceros smiled and went back to his drawing. He said nothing more.

Penguin Small floated out on the
wide ocean. He did not know
where he was, nor where he was going.
     The sky grew dark and big
drops of rain began to fall.

All night long the storm blew.
Penguin Small huddled in the
bottom of the Snowman's hat while the
waves tossed it high into the air and
sent it spinning round and round.

By morning the storm had passed.
Penguin Small found himself washed up
on a strange blue island.

'This is a very odd island' he said.
'It has no sand, no trees and no junglybirds
of any kind.'

But the island was not an island.
It was a great big blue…

WHOOSH!

Penguin Small found himself
flying through the air, flapping his
flippers furiously.
The Snowman's hat fell into the sea.
The scarf fluttered after it.
But Penguin Small…

Stayed right where he was!
Hovering in mid-air!
Squeaking at the top of his voice,
'I can fly! I can fly!'
      Then suddenly his wings got tired,
and he dropped like a floppy cushion
on to the Whale's nose.
      'Did you see?' he panted,
'I was flying!'

Soaring

The Whale was heading south to cold waters. He was used to travelling the oceans alone, but he was happy for Penguin Small to ride along with him.

While the Whale swam Penguin Small practised his flying, landing on the Whale's nose when he needed a rest.

As the days passed he became an expert...

Diving

They travelled far to the south.
The air became cold and icebergs began
to float by.

One day, climbing high in the sky,
Penguin Small spotted land. Looking
down he saw little shapes, just like
himself, lined up along the shore.

'Penguins!' he squeaked.

Way below him the Whale launched
himself clean out of the water!

The Whale landed in the sea, with a boom like a crack of thunder! Then he slid beneath the waves, flapping goodbyes with his enormous tail.

With a whoop of delight Penguin Small soared into the air,

looped the loop...

There never talked a snowman
Nor penguin ever flew
And there Neverwozanoceros
To make this rhyme for you.

The Neverwozanoceros